Alicia's Tutu

Robin Pulver * *paintings by* Mark Graham

For Nancy Mead's second grade

DANCE WITH WORDS!

Robin Pulver
1999

Dial Books for Young Readers *New York*

Published by Dial Books for Young Readers
A Division of Penguin Books USA Inc.
375 Hudson Street
New York, New York 10014

Designed by Nancy R. Leo
Printed in Hong Kong
First Edition
1 3 5 7 9 10 8 6 4 2

Library of Congress Cataloging in Publication Data
Pulver, Robin.
Alicia's tutu / Robin Pulver; paintings by Mark Graham.
p.   cm.
Summary: Alicia is convinced that a tutu will make her
a better dancer, but her mother says she doesn't need one.
ISBN 0-8037-1932-9 (trade)—ISBN 0-8037-1933-7 (lib.)
[1. Ballet dancing—Fiction. 2. Grandmothers—Fiction.]
I. Graham, Mark, date, ill. II. Title.
PZ7.P97325Al 1997   [E]—dc20   96-24503   CIP   AC

The art was prepared using oil paint on rag bristol paper.

That baby Josh is two and a half and such a climber! He somersaulted from his crib last night when Mom was watching me dance.

"I really need a tutu for my dancing, Mom," I said for the hundred-millionth time.

But all she said was, "It's time Josh had a bed like yours, Alicia."

Now, just as I'm pouring milk on my breakfast cereal, the telephone rings.

I can tell it's Grandma calling when Mom says, "Mother! We were just discussing that last night." She hands me the phone.

"Alicia," Grandma says, "I'm sending you a present."

"What kind of present?"

"Something you need," she says.

To myself I think, The only thing I absolutely need in this whole wide world is a tutu that's pink and pouffy and sparkly. I've needed a tutu like that ever since Grandma took me to see a real ballet.

Happiness bursts inside me. "When's the present coming, Grandma?"

"It should arrive by truck on Saturday. I hope it's not too big for you. By the way, I hope you're still dancing?"

"Oh, yes," I assure her. "My class is today."

After Grandma and I say good-bye, I tell Mom, "Grandma's sending me a tutu!"

"Oh, I don't think so," says Mom. "Didn't she tell you? She's sending you the bed and some other things from her guest room. You know she's moving to an apartment. She won't have room for all that furniture."

"Grandma would not call a bed a present," I say. "Something I *need* is what she said."

"That's right," Mom tells me. "And you need Grandma's bed so that Josh can have yours. In the spring you'll need a tutu for your recital. But right now you do not *need* a tutu. You *want* a tutu. There's a difference. Now eat up your cereal."

Then Mrs. Gregory, our sitter, comes. Mom scoops Josh and me into one big hug before she rushes off to her job at the clinic.

After school it's time for ballet class. First Mrs. Gregory and I deliver Josh to his friend Andrew's house, down the street. I can't believe all the toys at that house! Josh yells, "Choo choo!" and heads straight for the toy train. Not only is Josh a climber, he's crazy about trucks and trains and anything with wheels.

At my dance school I tell everyone in the changing room about my tutu. That girl Jolene, who always wears her hair in a dumb bun, says so what, she already has two tutus. But good old Molly says she can't wait to see mine. So I tell Molly how much I absolutely love her glittery nail polish.

Ms. Shirley has us practice our positions and our pliés and our chassés. Then we do a dance pretending we are tiny dancers inside music boxes. I pretend I'm wearing my tutu. It helps my dancing a lot.

At the end of class Ms. Shirley chooses Jolene to be queen, and we all have to bow and curtsy to her. I was hoping to be queen. Ms. Shirley taps me on the head. "Point that toe, Alicia!"

After dinner I find Mom stretched out on the couch. "Mom," I say, "Jolene has two tutus and she got to be queen today. Josh is the one who needs a bed. The only thing *I* need is a tutu. I'm sure that's what Grandma's sending."

"Oh dear," says Mom. "It's too bad Grandma called it a present. A bed is what she's sending."

My foot stomps. "Tutu tutu tutu!"

Mom stares at me with serious eyes. "Alicia, every day at the clinic I see children who need enough food to eat and better places to live. Please don't let me hear another word from you about needing a tutu."

I think, Maybe all those children need tutus too.

Saturday afternoon Josh toddles to the window and squeals, "See tuck! See tuck!"

Whewee! That is some big tutu delivery truck. Two men jump out of the truck to pull back the doors and unload the tutu. I'm so excited, I can't watch anymore. I run to the door, squeeze my eyes shut, and get ready for those men to deliver my tutu to me.

"Excuse us, miss," says a voice that's rough and polite at the same time.

"Yes?" I hear a shake in my voice. I keep my eyes closed tight and hold out my arms for the tutu.

"Can you show us where this bed is supposed to go?"

BED!

My eyes pop open. Grandma must have been joking about a present! But this joke is not funny! A bed is not what I need! This is all Josh's fault for being such a climber.

Mom says, "That bed goes in the room at the top of the stairs. Can you put it together for us? And please move the bed that is already in my daughter's room to the baby's room."

"Sure thing," says one of the men. "As soon as we bring in the rest of the stuff."

"What rest of the stuff?" I ask. "Is there a tutu?"

"Two what?" says the moving man. "Oh yeah, two more things. Besides the mattress."

They lug in a dresser and a vanity with a mirror on top. And finally a big mattress for the bed.

But no tutu.

I thought Grandma, of all people, would know that I need a tutu. I press my fists against my eyes to keep the tears in. Dancers don't usually cry.

Mom sits down on the stairs next to me. "Sweetheart, I know you were hoping for a tutu. You just have to be patient until recital time."

Josh tugs on my hand. "Weecia pway choo choo?"

"Go away, Josh," I say.

The moving men carry my perfectly fine bed into Josh's room. When they drive away at last, it's starting to get dark outside.

"Alicia!" calls Mom, "where's your brother?"

"Right here," I say. But he's not. We look and look just everywhere, calling all the time. Under the beds, in the closets, all around the bushes outside the house.

Josh is such a climber. And he loves trucks. What if he climbed into that moving truck and the moving men didn't know it?

Mom telephones the moving company to stop the truck. Her eyes look terrible.

All I can think about is Josh. Where could he be, oh, where could he be? My heart hurts with not knowing. I don't even care about the tutu anymore.

Then I remember, Josh wanted to play choo choo. I remember the toy train at Andrew's house.

"Mom, I think he's at Andrew's house!"

Mom and I run down the street and sure enough, there's Josh on Andrew's dark front porch, with his face pressed up against the window. When he sees us, he jumps up and down. "Weecia! Dere choo choo is!" I've got a hold of his hand, and Mom grabs him up.

Josh says with his sweetest little-boy voice, "Weecia want choo choo?"

Then suddenly I understand everything. "Oh, Josh, not choo choo, *tutu!* Were you trying to find the choo choo to make me happy? No, no! Tutu!"

Mom and I look at each other and at Josh and we laugh and hug all the way home.

Mom spreads clean sheets and a flowery quilt over the bed Grandma sent. Then she takes Josh to tuck him into the bed that used to be mine.

I sit on the big new bed and dangle my feet over the side. I lie flat on the bed. I bounce on the bed.

I stand up on the bed and watch
myself twirl in the vanity mirror.
Actually, this could be an okay bed
for a dancer.

Mom brings a pile of clean laundry
for me to put away in the new dresser.

I start that boring job. Underwear and socks in the top drawer. The middle drawer will be for my jeans. But what's this? All pink and crinkly and sparkly, stuffed in here? It's kind of like . . . a lot like . . .

"MOM! COME FAST!"

She comes running, looking scared. But then she sees what I see. She finds a note attached and reads out loud:

> "Dear Alicia,
>
> Remember to bring this the next time you visit. My new apartment has a nice wood floor for dancing. Sweet dreams, hon!
>
> Love, Grandma"

"Thank you, Grandma," I whisper as I put on the tutu. It's not too big. It's perfect.

I check to make sure Josh is safe and sound asleep. Then I pull Mom outside with me. I wonder what Grandma can see from her new apartment window. Can she see the stars twinkle as they bow and curtsy to the dancing queen?